A Game Is a Game —Or Is It?

by Dina Anastasio
illustrated by Lyn Boyer

Buff Goes Wild!

by Amanda Jenkins
illustrated by Shawn Byous

TWO REALISTIC FICTION STORIES

Table of Contents

Realistic Fiction

What is realistic fiction?

Realistic fiction features characters and plots that could actually happen in everyday life. The settings are authentic—they are based on familiar places such as a home, school, office, or farm. The stories involve some type of conflict, or problem. The conflict can be something a character faces within himself, an issue between characters, or a problem between a character and nature.

What is the purpose of realistic fiction?

Realistic fiction shows how people grow and learn, deal with successes and failures, make decisions, build relationships, and solve problems. In addition to making readers think and wonder, realistic fiction is entertaining. Most of us enjoy "escaping" into someone else's life for a while.

How do you read realistic fiction?

First, note the title. The title will give you a clue about an important character or conflict in the story. As you read, pay attention to the thoughts, feelings, and actions of the main characters. Note how the characters change from the beginning of the story to the end. Ask yourself: *What moves this character to action? Can I learn something from his or her struggles?*

Features of Realistic Fiction

The story takes place in an authentic setting.

At least one character deals with a conflict (self, others, or nature).

The characters are like people you might meet in real life.

The story is told from a first-person or third-person point of view.

Who tells the story in realistic fiction?

Authors usually write realistic fiction in one of two ways. In the first-person point of view, one of the characters tells the story as it happens to him or her, using words such as **I**, **me**, **my**, **mine**, **we**, **us**, and **our**. In the third-person point of view, a narrator tells the story, using words such as **he**, **she**, **they**, **their**, and the proper names of the characters.

Verbal Irony

Verbal irony is a figure of speech authors use when they intentionally want to express the opposite of what they say. When a car gets stuck in the mud, for instance, and the driver says, "That's just great," the driver doesn't really mean getting stuck in the mud is great. He means the opposite. Verbal irony adds emotional depth to stories because the reader has to put himself into the character's situation. The reader sees himself as the character and "hears" the dialogue in characters' voices.

Descriptive Language: Adjectives and Adverbs

Authors want readers to see, feel, smell, touch, and taste everything through written words. They also want readers to identify with characters' actions. To accomplish this task, authors include descriptive language in the form of adjectives and adverbs. Sound, smell, speed, time, and distance adjectives describe characters' actions and story setting. Adverbs also describe characters' actions by showing how, where, when, and how often things are done.

Sequence of Events

Good authors write stories with key events, or plot points, occurring in the beginning, the middle, and the end. These events are logically placed, creating a story's natural flow and rhythm. To help readers better understand a story's sequence, and connect one action or scene to another, authors often include key words and phrases such as **on** (date), **not long after**, **finally**, **when**, **as**, and **before**. Good readers look for a story's natural progression of events to help them better understand the plot.

Meet the Characters

Cave Adventures

Summer has finally arrived. Linda and her brother Jake have been coming to the same cabin on this rocky beach since they were little. Their friend Maria is back for her second summer. Cai is new to the seacoast. This summer promises new adventures since Linda and Jake's dad recently discovered a hidden cave.

Linda is a big talker with big ideas. She loves technology and gadgets, and hates that the cabins do not get TV reception or the Internet.

Jake is a smart boy who enjoys playing tricks and shooting hoops on the basket outside the cabin.

Maria is an only child. She lives with her divorced mother. She likes to bake and cook, and usually has her nose in a book.

Cai is spending the summer with his grandma. He likes to swim, fish, and play with his dog Tucker.

Oak Street Kids

Five kids couldn't be more different than Jalissa, Jamal, Brooke, Luke, and Tia. But they have some things in common, too! They all live in the Oak Street Apartments. They all have parents who work during the day. They are in the same after-school "club" run by the manager of the apartment building, Ms. Tilly. That's why the Oak Street Kids have made a deal: They will always stick together and help one another.

Jalissa likes drama and excitement, and is Jamal's twin sister.

Jamal is calm and easygoing, the opposite of his twin sister.

Brooke can always be counted on to organize and take charge.

Luke may not be a top student, but he's loyal and fun.

Tia loves every kind of sport.

Ms. Tilly is the no-nonsense manager of the Oak Street Apartments and takes care of the kids after school.

About the Settings

Cave Adventures

Dina Anastasio:
When I was a child, my sister, cousins, and I spent our summers at my grandparents' cabin on a lake. We spent our days

jumping off the end of the dock, swimming out to the raft, and exploring mysterious places with friends from other cabins.

A few years ago, I discovered a place in Camden, Maine, that brought back fond memories of my grandparents' cabin. I have gone back to these cabins on the seacoast often, in part because it makes me feel connected to the "home away from home" I loved so much. There is no dock or raft to swim to, but there are caves to explore, and many of the same families return every summer. These caves, located near the water, served as the inspiration for the setting of the "Cave Adventures" stories.

Oak Street Kids

Amanda Jenkins: Like the Oak Street Kids, I lived in a garden apartment growing up in Fort Worth, Texas. There were good things and bad things about it. One bad thing was that I wasn't supposed to run and jump inside. Our apartment was upstairs, so our floor was someone else's ceiling!

One of the best things was that all kinds of kids lived there. Somebody was always playing outside, so I could just run out and join in. We played in courtyards and on patios, under stairs and along sidewalks.

A Game Is a Game —Or Is It?

It was one of those dark, drizzly summer days when there's nothing to do but hang out at home. Cai and I were playing Scrabble® on my screened-in porch. I was a few points behind, so I was concentrating extra-hard on my letters. Cai was being politely silent, but his dog Tucker sure wasn't. Tucker was sleeping **nearby**, tossing and turning and snorting and snoring and making it extremely hard to focus on possible *Z* and *J* words.

I was about to lay down the word "dazes" for 20 points when Jake and Linda strolled by in their rain jackets. They were looking at each other, and I guess they didn't notice us because Jake said, in a very loud voice, "Why would I want Cai? He's a terrible player!"

I glanced up to see if Cai was okay; he was. He just shrugged off Jake's rudeness and continued staring at the Scrabble® board.

Jake and Linda had stopped walking. They were facing the water so their backs were to us.

"I'm not sure you realize that I'm a great basketball player," Jake was saying. "Michael Jordan has nothing on me! I have **whirlwind** moves so playing one-on-one against you is no kind of a challenge. I've tried to teach you, Linda, but you don't listen!"

"Maybe I'd listen better if you'd stop yelling at me," Linda said.

"Well, anyway, I wish there were better players around."

"How about Maria and me against you and Cai?" Linda suggested.

"Cai? You're kidding! Suggesting I play on the same team as Cai makes me laugh. *Har-dee-har-har.* I've told you ten times that I refuse to play on a team with Cai. He is worse than horrendous. He is so deeply uncoordinated that he is a liability. He could even make me lose. Maria isn't about to make any school team either, but she's better than Cai. Hey, I know! I'll play against you and Maria, and Cai can do something he's good at, like read."

I could tell that Cai was beginning to feel sad because his shoulders were slumping lower and lower, and he moved close to Tucker and was petting him like he usually did when he needed a friend.

I decided it might be best to add a little humor so I said, "Good old Jake. Always so kind."

Cai managed a reluctant smile and shrugged. I didn't know what else to say to make him feel better so I shouted at Jake. "Hey! We're right here you know, listening to everything you're saying."

Jake and Linda swung around. Jake's eyes were wide and embarrassed, but he didn't apologize. He just stood there, gaping at us.

Cai mumbled something about it being okay, and then he grabbed his book and led Tucker up the beach toward the cave. Jake and Linda came onto the porch.

"You should look before you talk," I told Jake. "Especially if you're planning on saying something that's mean."

"Oh, come on!" Jake said. "He knows he can't play basketball. It's just not his thing like it is mine. And he certainly can't be surprised to hear he's uncoordinated."

"Oh, I'm sure he loved hearing that."

I was tired of Jake, and for the first time that summer, I felt like telling him so.

"Go away!" I said. "Leave me alone, and leave Cai alone, too."

"Fine!" he said, but I could tell my words had stunned him a little. I almost never yell at people, so I'm sure he realized that I was very angry.

Jake made a **hasty** retreat, and Linda called back to me, "Sorry," as she followed her brother out the door.

I stayed on the porch for a while because I couldn't decide whether I should go to the cave and comfort Cai or leave him alone. I must have been making a decision, because while I was thinking, I was packing up the Scrabble® set, and before I knew it, I was carrying the box up to the cave.

Cai was in a back corner with Tucker. He was reading a book with the flashlight we always keep in the cave and he didn't even look up when I came in. "Want to play another round?" I asked.

He nodded and closed his book and we set up the game together. As we played, we took turns shining the flashlight on the board. Nobody said anything until Tucker started barking and Linda said, "Hi." She was standing in the cave entrance with one foot in and one foot out like she wasn't sure if she should come in or not.

"Want to play?" Cai asked her.

"Sure." Linda sat with us and waited as we finished our game.

I was surprised that Linda had agreed to play a board game. Linda's obsession is electronic games. Once I heard her say that there's nothing in the whole world she'd rather do than play games on her computer.

"You mean it?" I asked. "You really want to play?"

"Of course I do. Why not?"

Maybe she was being nice. Maybe she felt bad about what Jake had said. Or maybe she really was interested. It was hard to tell.

"Can you hear him?" Linda asked as Cai was trying to find a way to use his last two letters.

"Hear what?" I asked.

"Shh, listen. Jake is working out his feelings again."

We stopped playing and listened. Even Tucker was quiet. It took a while to hear what Linda had heard, but then we did hear it. It was the faint sound of Jake's basketball hitting the side of his cabin over and over again, at first hard and angry, then hesitant, then softly until the thuds slowed and stopped all together.

Cai went back to fumbling around with his letters until he finally played them and won the game.

We were setting up for another game when Jake appeared in the entrance. I was still annoyed about what he'd said about Cai, so I ignored him. But Cai didn't.

"We're playing Scrabble®," he said. "Would you like to play?" **Sometimes** I can hardly believe how nice Cai can be.

Jake shuffled his feet for a while and made a brief exit. He returned a few minutes later and mumbled, "No thanks," but this time he didn't leave. He just stood there, watching, as Cai and Linda and I started to play.

"You really like that game?" he asked no one in particular.

"I like word games a lot," Cai said. "They make you think of new words, and they make you use words you usually don't use. Word games are fun and a challenge. It's me versus the entire dictionary."

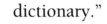

"Word games are stupid, for bab—"

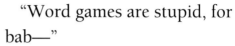

I knew Jake was going to say that word games are for babies, but he must have thought better of it because he stopped himself.

"Just ignore him," Linda said. "If we ignore him, he might go away, back to his 'adult' basketball game."

We tried to ignore Jake, but it wasn't easy. He kept clearing his throat and bouncing the ball loudly and trying to get our attention. We just kept playing and pretending he wasn't there.

"Oh, okay then," Jake groaned. "I'll say it if you want me to. Maybe board games aren't stupid or for babies. Maybe I'm just not any good at them. Maybe I'm terrible at board games. And, well, okay, I'm sorry."

I pointed the flashlight at him. "Some people are good at board games and some people are good at basketball," I said. "But I guess we can accept your **belated** apology, even though it doesn't sound like you mean it. What do you think, Cai?"

"Would you like us to teach you Scrabble®?" Cai asked.

Jake joined us, uneasily, using his basketball as a seat. "Okay, I'm ready to learn," he announced. "And maybe when we're done, I can teach you how to sink a basket. A favor for a favor."

"Lucky us!" I said. The idea of Jake teaching us basketball made me angry again.

"No thanks," Cai said. He didn't sound angry at all. He just sounded definite, like he was done pretending that he enjoyed basketball.

"I know how you teach," Linda added. "And it isn't very pleasant."

Jake looked crumpled up, like he had shrunk. I had to think for a while before I could sort out and explain what was on my mind.

Jake sat there, fumbling with his letters; it was clear that he had no idea what to do. Then Cai calmly helped him out.

"If we take your letters *T* and *H*, then use the *R* in this word here and add *I*, *L*, and *L*, we make the word *thrill*."

"Is this fun?" Jake asked. I wondered if he was talking to himself.

"For me it is," Cai told him, which made me understand exactly what to say.

"As I mentioned earlier, Jake, some people are good at board games and some people are good at basketball. Don't take it **personally**, but I think that Cai and I are happily going to stick to board games and leave shooting baskets to you."

Reread the Story

Analyze the Characters, Setting, and Plot

- Who are the main characters in this story?
- What are Cai and Maria doing at the beginning of the story?
- What are Linda and Jake doing at the beginning of the story?
- What does Jake do that causes a problem?
- What do we learn about Jake? What do we learn about Cai?
- How does the story end?

Focus on Comprehension: Sequence of Events

- What does Maria do right after Jake says Cai certainly can't be surprised to hear that he's uncoordinated?

- What happens right before Jake appears at the entrance to the cave?

- What does Jake say after he is ignored by his friends in the cave?

Analyze the Tools Writers Use:
Verbal Irony

- On page 9, Jake says, "You're kidding! Suggesting I play on the same team as Cai makes me laugh. *Har-dee-har-har*." Why is this an example of verbal irony?

- On page 10, Maria tells Jake, "Oh, I'm sure he loved hearing that." Would Cai really love hearing that he's uncoordinated? What does Maria mean by saying this?

- On page 14, Maria says, "Lucky us!" Does she feel lucky? If she doesn't feel lucky, what does she feel?

Focus on Words: Descriptive Language

Make a chart like the one on the next page. Read each descriptive word in the chart. Identify if it is an adjective or an adverb and then identify what it describes. Next, analyze the adjectives and adverbs. What do these adjectives and adverbs have in common?

Page	Word	Adjective or Adverb	What It Describes
8	nearby		
9	whirlwind		
11	hasty		
12	sometimes		
13	belated		
15	personally		

Buff Goes Wild!

O
h no!" groaned Jamal. "This is just great." He stood in the doorway of his family's apartment, looking in despair at the mess in the living room. White cotton fluff lay everywhere, strewn like little clouds on the carpet. One of the throw pillows that usually sat on the couch was now a flat, empty sack lying in the middle of the floor. One corner of it had been chewed off.

Jamal stepped inside, shutting the front door behind him. "Buff!" he called as he strode around looking for his dog. "Where are you?" It was the third day this week he'd come home from school to find that Buff had destroyed something.

"Our apartment isn't very large," Jamal's mom had told him **yesterday**, after he had **reluctantly** showed her a shoe that Buff had chewed to pieces. "We need to consider whether this is really the best home for a big dog. Maybe we should give Buff to a family who has a house with a yard."

The thought of losing his dog had made Jamal's chest ache. "This is the best home for Buff!" he had protested. "We're his family!"

But Jamal's mother had looked doubtful, and Jamal knew that Buff was in danger of being sent away. This morning, Jamal had gone through the apartment carefully putting away everything a dog might want to chew on.

Readers can tell this is realistic fiction because the story takes place in a familiar setting, an apartment. Note that the author is using the third-person point of view.

The author introduces the problem. Buff may need to find a new home. What can Jamal do to prevent that from happening?

19

But Buff had found something to tear up anyway. "There you are!" Jamal said as he spotted Buff trying unsuccessfully to hide behind a bed.

Jamal dropped to his knees beside a cowering Buff. "It's all right, boy," he assured the dog, "I'm not going to scold you." Jamal had already tried scolding, and it didn't work. "I just want to know why do you keep doing this when you know it'll get you into trouble?"

Buff licked Jamal's face, which was his way of answering the question.

Jamal cleaned up the cottony mess and then took Buff on a short walk. This was part of their daily routine; each morning, Mom went to work while Jamal and his twin sister Jalissa walked to school with the other kids from the Oak Street Apartments. After school Jalissa, Brooke, Luke, and Tia came straight to Ms. Tilly's apartment, but Jamal always slipped quickly upstairs to get Buff and take him outside before bringing him to Ms. Tilly's.

Today Buff was his usual happy self on his walk. He sniffed things, saw people, and greeted other dogs with a wagging tail and a relaxed, slobbery grin. When he came into Ms. Tilly's apartment,

20

he collapsed on the floor with a tired, satisfied snort and immediately went to sleep.

Jamal brought his homework to the dining table and sat down with the other kids. He let out a sad-sounding sigh as he opened his math book. "Don't tell me," Jalissa said, "Buff did it again."

The author's use of descriptive language about Jamal's sigh tells readers how the character is feeling.

"He ripped up another couch pillow," Jamal agreed gloomily.

The other kids exchanged sympathetic looks; they knew about the problems with Buff. "I need help," Jamal confessed. "I've got to get Buff to behave—and quickly—or else!"

The author develops the problem. Buff continues to destroy things in the apartment. Jamal is getting more worried.

Everyone immediately started thinking hard: *How do you get a dog to stop tearing things up?*

In the silence, Luke's pencil began to tap rapidly on the tabletop. *Rat-a-tat-rat-a-tat-rat-a-tat.*

"Can you please be quiet?" Brooke asked.

Luke looked down at his pencil in surprise. "Sorry," he said, "I didn't notice."

"How can you not notice that you're making a noise like a woodpecker?" Tia wondered.

"I don't know," Luke said, "I don't mean to aggravate people."

"This is a no-tapping zone!" Jalissa told him. "It's a thinking zone!"

In this exchange of dialogue, the author reveals Luke's character. The reader also learns about Luke from his actions. How his friends react and what they say to Luke tell about their personalities, too.

"All I can think is that I feel bad for Buff," said Luke. "If it were me sitting around an apartment all day with nothing to do, I'd be bored silly."

"Hey, maybe that's the problem," said Jamal, "maybe Buff is bored. In that case, I just need to find him something to do."

"You could leave the TV on for him," said Luke.

"Dogs don't watch television," Brooke informed him.

"Buy Buff some toys to keep him busy," Tia suggested to Jamal.

"I'm broke," Jamal said glumly. "I used up my allowance replacing the stuff Buff already chewed up."

"I've got some money," said Tia. "I'll buy him a toy."

"Me, too," the other kids chimed in.

"Thanks," Jamal said gratefully.

Ms. Tilly agreed to walk the kids to the pet store, where they purchased an assortment of dog toys. Jalissa bought a stuffed squirrel with shaggy, neon-green fur. Tia bought a miniature football. Luke bought a rubber bone that turned out to have a really annoying squeaker inside. Practical Brooke bought a bin to keep all the toys in so they wouldn't be scattered all over the apartment and bother Jamal's mom.

The next morning before leaving for school, Jamal made sure Buff had all his new toys with him. And in the afternoon after school, the other kids came along to see how Buff had behaved.

"*Ugh! Gack!*" Tia said as she stepped inside the apartment.

"What is that **putrid** smell?" shouted Jalissa.

"*Pee-yew!*" Luke said. "Something stinks."

The author develops the plot and shows each character's personality by what they get for Buff.

Another way to tell that this is realistic fiction is by the way the characters speak. They use the same words and fun expressions that kids use when they are with friends.

23

With a sinking heart, Jamal led the way to the kitchen. This time Buff had gotten into the closed garbage can and dragged out all the trash. The **acrid** scent of old onion peels mixed with the **noxious** odor of sour milk. Worst of all, Jamal's aunt had visited last night with her new baby, and a used disposable diaper lay in the middle of the floor.

The conflict continues to develop and gets more serious. The characters' solution to buy Buff toys has not worked. The author has made Jamal a likable character that the readers will root for. They will keep reading to find out if Jamal will have to give his dog away.

"Wonderful," said Jamal, "this is just what I needed."

Buff huddled in a corner, his head down in shame.

"I know how you feel, buddy," Luke told Buff as the kids helped Jamal clean up the **reeking** mess. "People are always getting aggravated with me, too."

24

When the kids got back to Ms. Tilly's apartment, they gathered around the table, determined to come up with another solution. Buff went into Ms. Tilly's office and took a nap at her feet.

At first the dining room was silent while everyone thought, but after a few moments a noise started—a low, vibrating rattle. Everyone looked around, trying to figure out what it was.

As the noise increased, the books and papers on the table began to quiver.

"It's Luke!" Jalissa cried. "He's jiggling his leg, and it's making the whole table shake!"

"I can't help it!" Luke protested. "At school I have to sit still for hours and hours, and then I come here and I have to sit all over again! It's torture!"

The other kids felt a twinge of sympathy; they knew that Luke often got into trouble at school for not paying attention or making too much noise.

"It's not your fault," said Brooke. "You've just got a lot of pent-up energy."

"Go run around the courtyard," Jamal suggested. "Burn some of it off."

Luke called eagerly to Ms. Tilly, "Can I?"

"Yes," Ms. Tilly called back grumpily. "Please do."

Luke leaped to his feet, knocking his chair over with a crash. "Sorry," he said, and picked it up. The next moment he was gone, slamming the door after him.

The other kids settled in again, trying to think.

"It sure is quiet without Luke in here," observed Tia.

Brooke agreed. "I'm so used to him making noise that now I can't think."

Jamal, meanwhile, was concentrating on his own problem. "We were on the right track with the toys," he said. "If only we can manage to see this from Buff's perspective, we'll understand why he tears things up."

Jalissa slipped out of her chair and got down on her hands and knees.

"What are you doing?" asked Tia.

"I'm looking at the world from a dog's perspective," Jalissa answered. "*Hmm*. For one thing, dogs are very short."

The door slammed again as Luke came back, his face flushed from exercise. "That was a good idea, Jamal. Thanks." He sat down at the table.

Silence fell again. Luke didn't fidget at all now. It was awfully quiet.

"Hey!" Jamal sat up in his chair. "That's it!"

"What? What?" everyone asked.

The kids' conversation and actions give Jamal an idea about how to solve Buff's problem.

"I'll burn off Buff's energy before I leave in the morning," Jamal explained. "Tomorrow I'll get up early and take him for a walk before school—no, a run! Then he won't have any pent-up energy, and he'll be able to get through the day without tearing stuff up!"

Jamal solves the problem! He will apply Luke's strategy to "burn off energy" with Buff.

The next day, Jamal set his alarm early and carried out his plan. After school, all the kids trooped up the stairs to see whether Buff had behaved himself.

Jamal opened the door to an expanse of clean, empty carpet.

No strewn trash. No gutted pillows. No chewed-up shoes. Just a relaxed Buff, who came to greet the kids, wagging his tail happily.

"Tomorrow morning I'm coming with you two," Luke told Jamal as he patted Buff on the head. "If a run before school helps Buff, maybe it'll help me, too."

Jamal grinned. It seemed that looking at things from someone else's point of view could solve all kinds of problems.

27

Analyze the Characters, Setting, and Plot

- Who are the main characters in this story?
- What is the problem in this story?
- Describe Buff. What kind of dog is he? How does he behave toward people?
- How do the kids try to help with the problem? Do their efforts work?
- How are Jamal and Buff alike?
- How does Jamal solve the problem?
- How does the story end?

Focus on Comprehension: Sequence of Events

- What does Jamal do first thing every afternoon before he goes to Ms. Tilly's apartment?

- What does Jamal do before leaving for school?

- What is the last thing Jamal tries to do to keep Buff from destroying things?

Focus on Perspective

Perspective is the way in which objects appear. Grade-school children see things much differently from toddlers because of the obvious height differences and what they know about the world. When is perspective used in this story? How is it used? How does the change in perspective help solve the problem?

Analyze the Tools Writers Use: Verbal Irony

- On page 19, Jamal says, "This is just great." He is talking about the mess that Buff made. How is this statement an example of verbal irony?

- On page 21, Jalissa says, "Don't tell me." Does she really not want to be told what Buff did? Why did she say this?

- On page 24, Jamal says, "Wonderful, this is just what I needed." Do Buff's actions make Jamal feel wonderful? If he doesn't feel wonderful, what does he feel?

Focus on Words: Descriptive Language

Make a chart like the one below. Read each descriptive word in the chart. Identify if it is an adjective or an adverb and then identify what it describes. Next, analyze the adjectives and adverbs. What do these adjectives and adverbs have in common?

Page	Word	Adjective or Adverb	What It Describes
19	yesterday		
19	reluctantly		
23	putrid		
24	acrid		
24	noxious		
24	reeking		

How does an author write

Realistic Fiction?

Reread "Buff Goes Wild!" and think about what Amanda Jenkins did to write this story. How did she develop it? How can you, as a writer, develop your own story?

1. Decide on a Problem

Remember, the characters in realistic fiction face the same problems you might face. In "Buff Goes Wild!" the problem is that a boy needs to get his big dog to stop destroying things—or the dog will be sent away.

Character	Jamal	Luke	Tia
Traits	responsible; problem-solver	sympathetic; energetic	thoughtful; generous
Examples	he takes Buff out for a walk before he takes him to Ms. Tilly's after school; he figures out that Buff needs to burn off excess energy and takes the dog for a long run every morning	Luke feels bad that Buff has nothing to do all day; Luke has trouble sitting still; he either taps his pencil or jiggles his leg	she comes up with the idea that Buff needs some toys; she offers to help pay for Buff's toys

Brainstorm Characters

Writers ask these questions:
- What kind of person will my main character be? What are his or her traits? Interests?
- What things are important to my main character? What does he or she want?
- What other characters will be important to my story? How will each one help or hinder the main character?
- How will the characters change? What will they learn about life?

 ## Brainstorm Setting and Plot

Writers ask these questions:
- Where does my story take place? How will I describe the setting?
- What is the problem, or situation?
- What events happen? How does the story end?
- Will my readers be entertained? Will they learn something?

Setting	the Oak Street Apartments
Problem of the Story	Jamal needs to get his big dog, Buff, to stop destroying things in his apartment.
Story Events	1. Buffs chews and destroys things in his apartment for three days in a row, which makes Jamal's mom think that maybe Buff needs to find a new home. 2. Jamal is determined to keep Buff and tries to figure out why the dog is acting out. 3. Jamal's friends help him think up a solution and they decide to buy Buff some toys to give him something to do during the day. 4. The toys don't do the trick. Buff is still destroying things. 5. Luke has so much pent-up energy that his friends tell him to go outside and work it off, and they realize that this is Buff's problem, too.
Solution to the Problem	Jamal takes Buff for a long run every morning before school to work off his energy, and the dog stops destroying things in the apartment during the day.

Glossary

acrid   (A-krid) unpleasant; caustic (page 24)

belated   (bih-LAY-ted) delayed; coming late (page 13)

hasty   (HAY-stee) speedy and impatient (page 11)

nearby   (neer-BY) not far away (page 8)

noxious   (NAHK-shus) harmful; obnoxious (page 24)

personally   (PER-suh-nuh-lee) as a judgment of one's character or motives (page 15)

putrid   (PYOO-trid) rotten; foul (page 23)

reeking   (REE-king) giving off an offensive odor (page 24)

reluctantly   (rih-LUK-tunt-lee) with hesitation (page 19)

sometimes   (SUM-timez) occasionally (page 12)

whirlwind   (WERL-wind) forceful and speedy (page 9)

yesterday   (YES-ter-day) on the day previous to today (page 19)